W9-BLR-849

For all those in search of their other half.

WWW.ENCHANTEDLIONBOOKS.COM

First edition published in 2016 by Enchanted Lion Books
351 Van Brunt Street, Brooklyn, NY 11231

A CIP record is on file with the Library of Congress
ISBN 978-1-59270-202-2

Book design: JooHee Yoon

Printed in China in May 2016 by
R.R. Donnelley Asia Print Solutions

The artwork in this book was created using
a combination of hand drawing, relief
printing, and the computer.

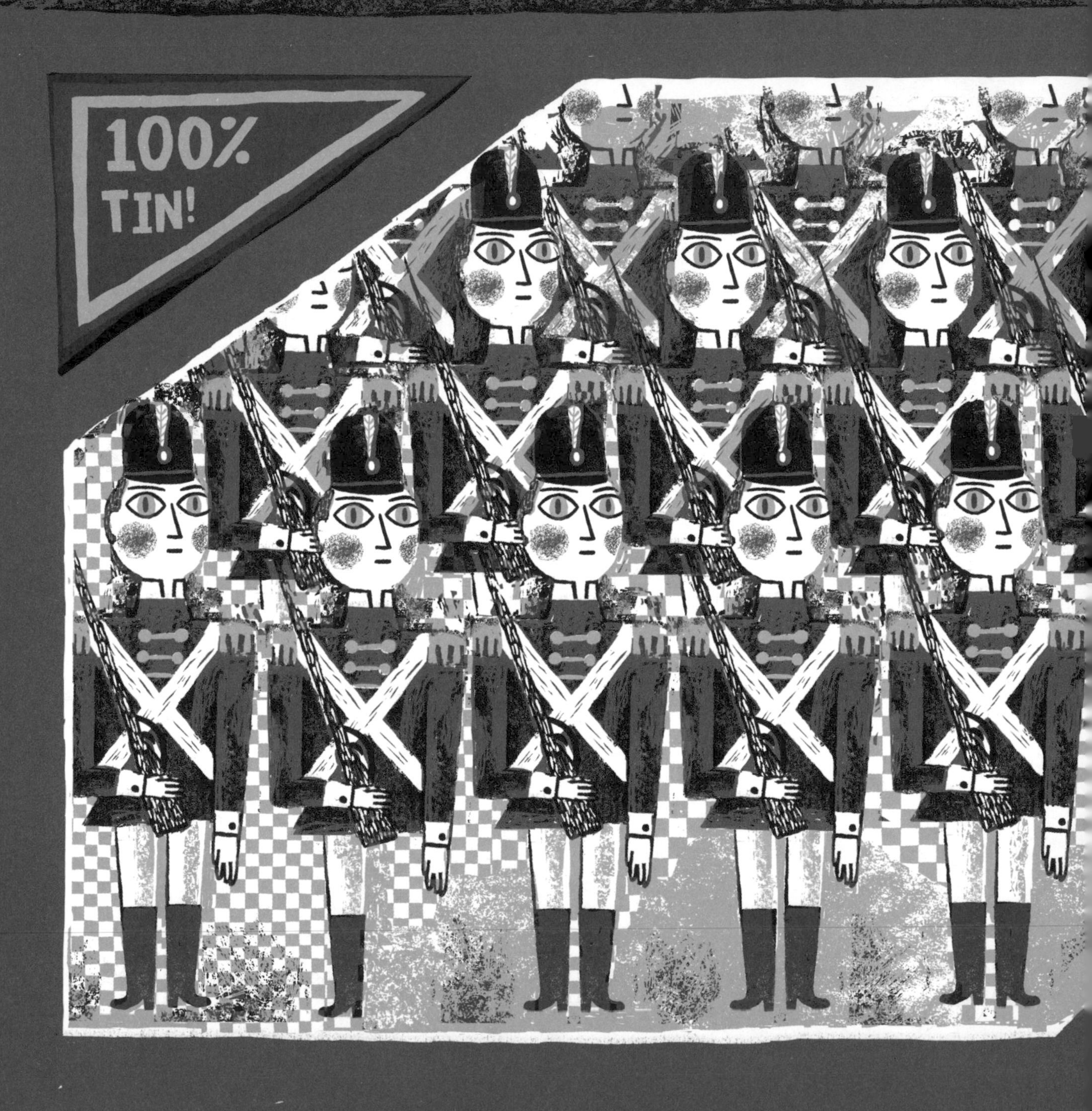
HANS CHRISTIAN
100% TIN!

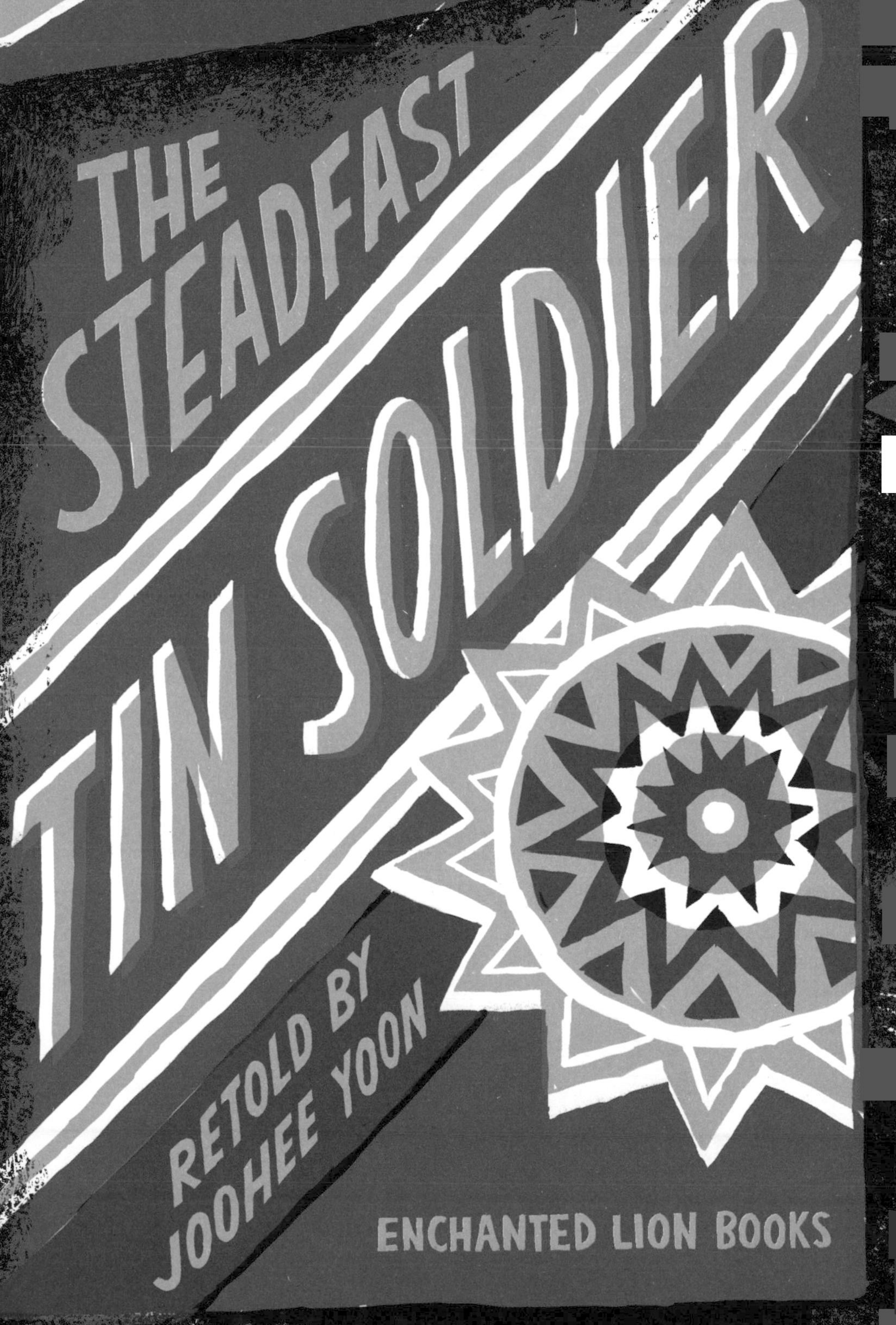
NDERSEN
THE STEADFAST
TIN SOLDIER
RETOLD BY
JOOHEE YOON
ENCHANTED LION BOOKS

Once there were five and twenty tin soldiers, all of them brothers, being made from the same tin spoon. Nestled in a box and wrapped in bright paper, they were given to a little boy who clapped with joy when he saw them. Each soldier was exactly like the next except for one, which was missing a leg, since there hadn't been enough melted tin to fill the last mold.

Yet the one-legged tin soldier stood just as well on his one leg as the others did on two.

This is his story.

In no time at all, the one-legged
tin soldier found himself
on the table where the
other toys lived.

In their midst, there stood a magnificent cardboard castle. It had a silver mirror for a lake, on which two wax swans floated, with miniature trees along its shores. But most marvelous of all was the lovely paper ballerina poised in the doorway. Her dress was of the softest muslin and she wore a ribbon fastened with a silver sequin as big as her face.

Balancing on tiptoe, with the other leg lifted, she appeared to the tin soldier to have only one leg.

“How graceful she is,” thought the tin soldier. “If only she could be my wife. Though I guess she is too grand for someone like me. After all, I live with my brothers in a box while she lives in a castle.”

Feeling shy, the tin soldier could only admire her from afar.

At day's end, when all the toys were put back in their proper places, the people of the house went to sleep.

Once the house was still and quiet,
the toys were free to play!

All the while, the ballerina remained upright, and the tin soldier stood just as faithfully.

Never once did his gaze
leave the ballerina.

When the clock struck midnight, a fearsome troll sprang from his box with a loud POP! He was in a terrible mood since he also admired the ballerina, but until now there had been no one to compete for her affections.

"Keep your eyes to yourself," the troll growled menacingly at the tin soldier. "Or else you will regret it!"

The tin soldier pretended not to hear, but this only made the troll angrier.

In the morning, the boy came down to play and happened to place his one-legged tin soldier on the window sill.

Whether it was a passing gust of wind or the troll's doing, no one can say, but an instant later, the tin soldier fell straight out of the window onto the hard, cold cobblestones far below.

The little boy went down to look, but failed to spot his soldier. If the tin soldier had called out, "Here I am!" he would have been found, but he thought it undignified to make a fuss.

To make matters worse, it began to rain. Soon it was a torrential downpour.

When the storm was over, two boys ran by with a paper boat. They had been on the lookout for a sailor to captain their ship when they spotted the tin soldier lying on the ground. They placed him inside their little boat and set him afloat in the gutter, which the recent rain had transformed into a miniature river.

The boat sailed swiftly along, pitching back and forth on the rough waters. At times it was impossible for the tin soldier to tell what was up and what was down, as the constant motion of the boat made his head spin. Inwardly he trembled with fear, but he stood firm, looking straight ahead.

Before long, the swirling waters carried the boat into the dark sewers.

As it happened, a large rat lived there. When he saw the soldier floating down, he tried to block his way and demanded, "Have you got a passport? Show me your passport!" But the tin soldier kept silent and the rat, who did not like to be ignored, got angrier still. "Stop him!" he squealed. "He hasn't got a passport." But as there was no one to heed his command, the rat had to let the soldier pass.

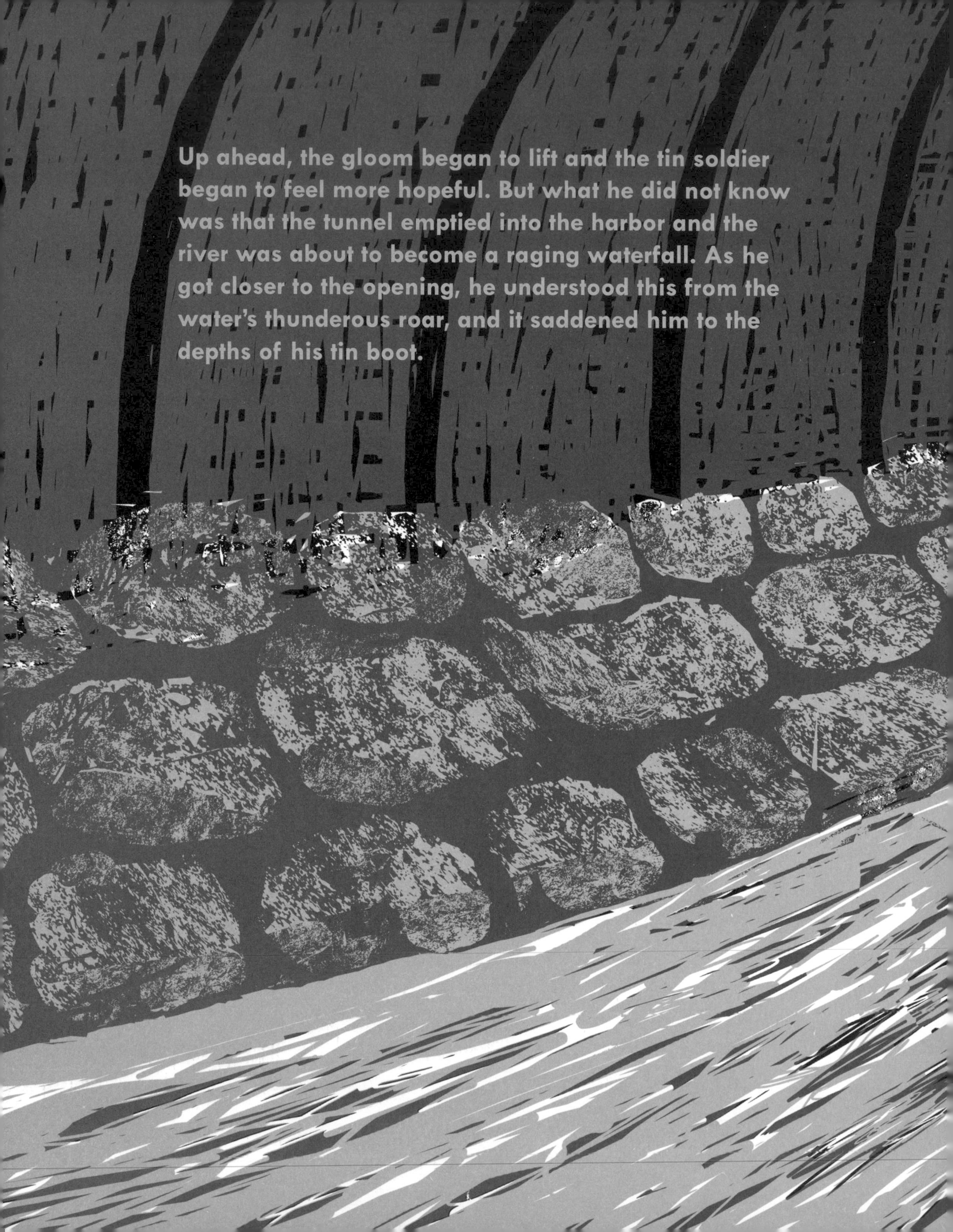

Up ahead, the gloom began to lift and the tin soldier began to feel more hopeful. But what he did not know was that the tunnel emptied into the harbor and the river was about to become a raging waterfall. As he got closer to the opening, he understood this from the water's thunderous roar, and it saddened him to the depths of his tin boot.

At that moment, the tin soldier felt certain that he would never see the ballerina again. But steadfast as ever, he was prepared to meet his fate with fortitude.

The paper boat tumbled into the rushing water, and the tin soldier reflected how very strange life is. He would never have imagined, not in a million years, that he would end up at sea. Plummeting down into the murky depths, he wondered what the ballerina was doing and whether the troll had won her heart.

The plunge was deep and the tin soldier would have been lost forever, if it hadn't been for a greedy fish who swallowed him in a single gulp.

How dark it was inside the fish!

But there were other greedy creatures roaming the seas.

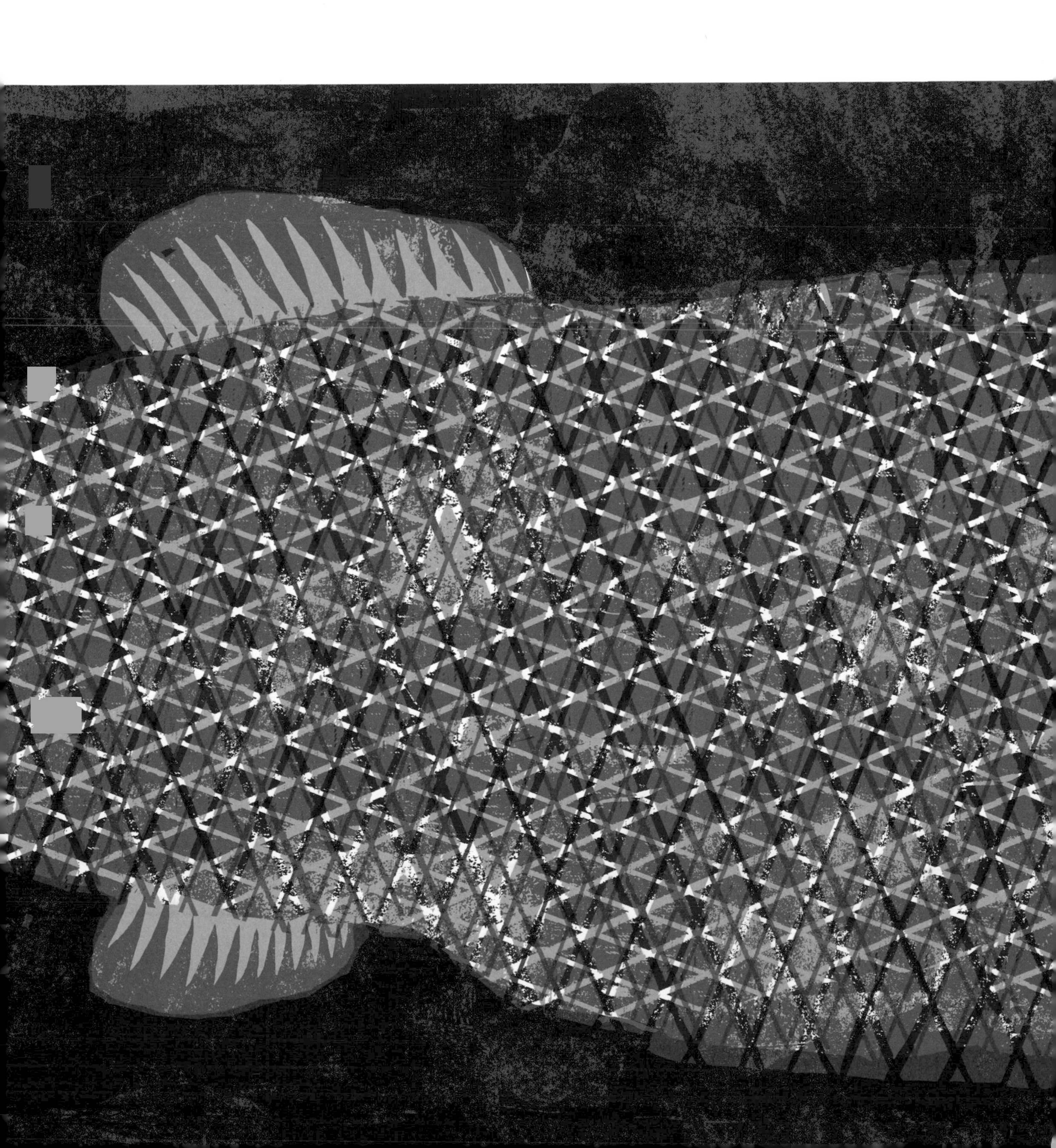

So it was that the fish which had swallowed the tin soldier ended up at market the next morning. There it caught the eye of a cook who thought it perfect for a nice stew.

But the cook was not just any cook. She was the very one who worked in the house where the little boy lived.

As soon as the cook brought the fish home, she began to clean it, thinking how tasty the stew would be with such a fat fish.

But these pleasant thoughts were interrupted...

...when she discovered the missing tin soldier right inside the fish!

Once she got over her initial shock, the cook scrubbed the tin soldier clean and placed him back on the table with the other toys.

When the tin soldier saw the ballerina again, he found her even more lovely than he remembered. There she stood, still on her one leg, as steady as he. The sight nearly made him weep tears of tin. But he kept back his tears and gazed at the ballerina in silent admiration, as she looked back at him.

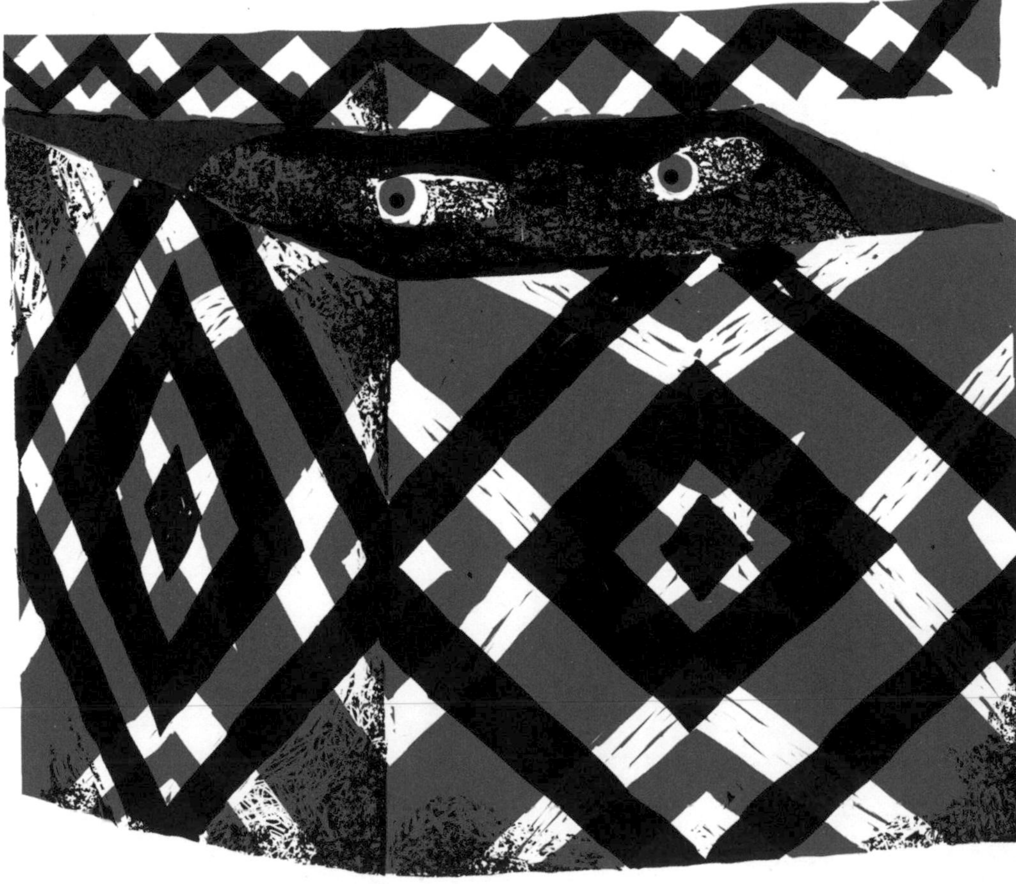

As for the troll, he was most unhappy to see the tin soldier again.

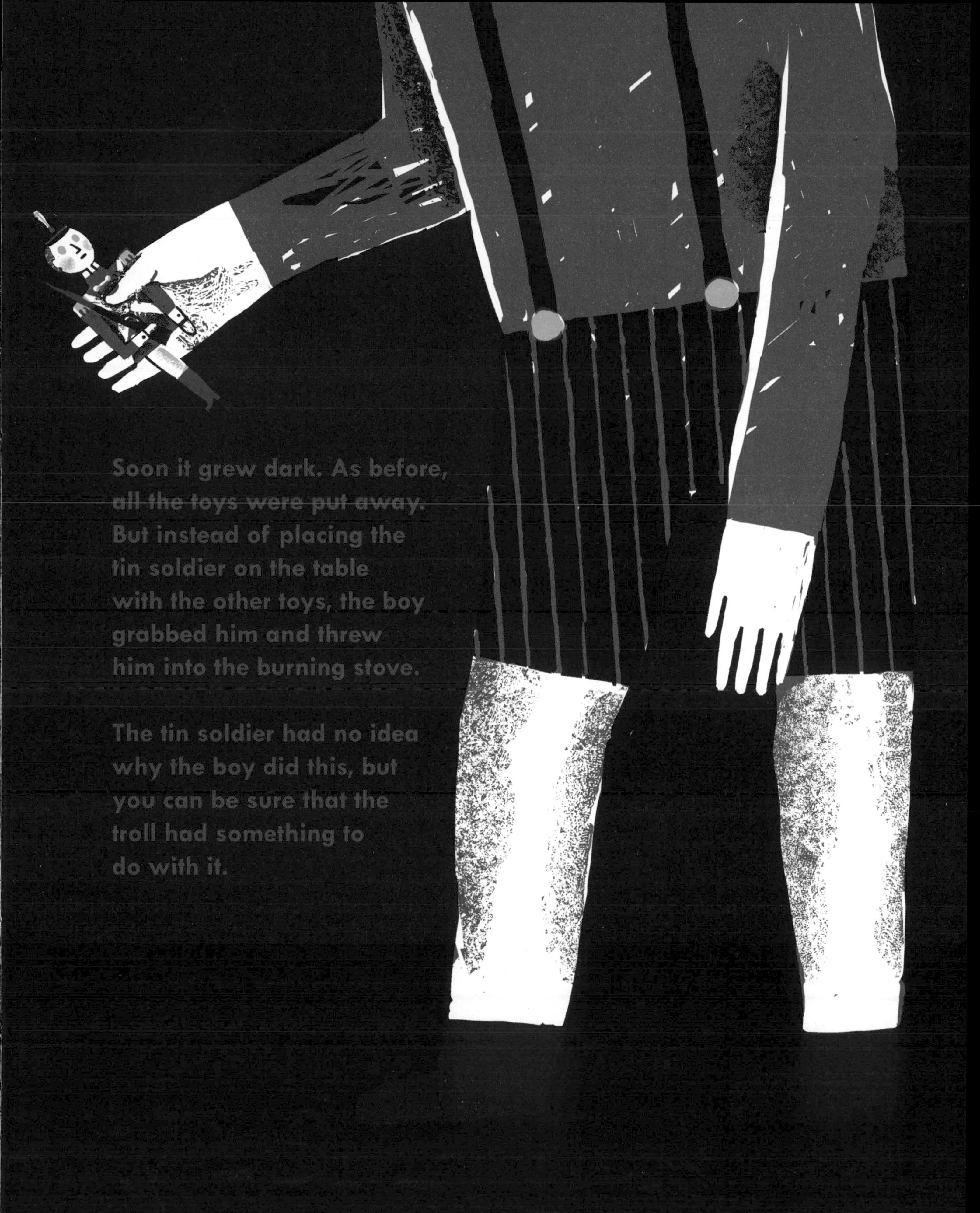

Soon it grew dark. As before, all the toys were put away. But instead of placing the tin soldier on the table with the other toys, the boy grabbed him and threw him into the burning stove.

The tin soldier had no idea why the boy did this, but you can be sure that the troll had something to do with it.

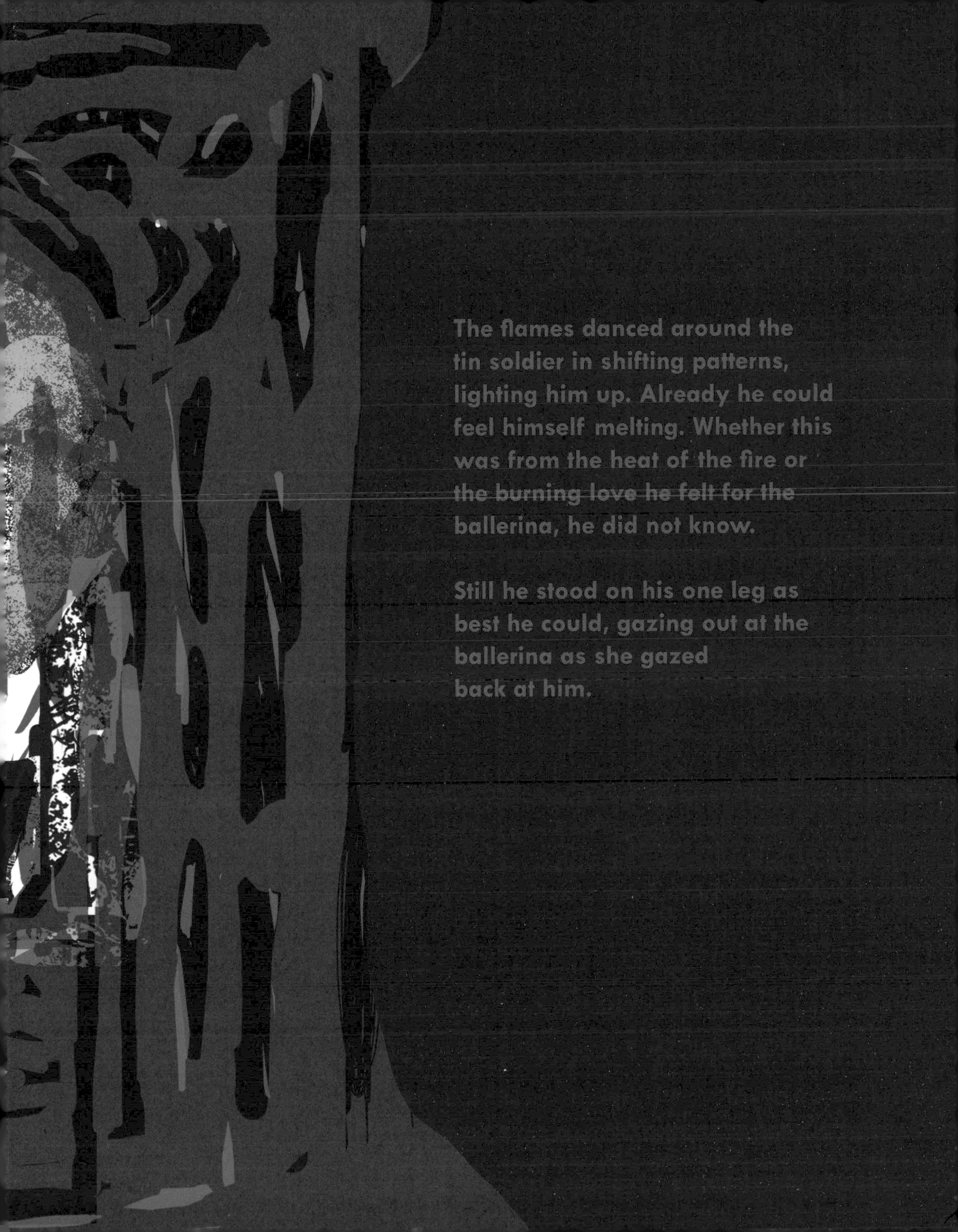

The flames danced around the tin soldier in shifting patterns, lighting him up. Already he could feel himself melting. Whether this was from the heat of the fire or the burning love he felt for the ballerina, he did not know.

Still he stood on his one leg as best he could, gazing out at the ballerina as she gazed back at him.

Just then the door to the room opened
and a breeze blew in, carrying the ballerina
straight towards the tin soldier and into the stove.

For the briefest of moments, they were together.

Then, in a flash, the flames reduced the paper
ballerina to ash. Soon after, the tin soldier
melted into a shimmering puddle.

In the morning, all that remained of the tin soldier and the ballerina were a heart-shaped lump of tin and a charred sequin.